BOOK WORMS

Earth Matters
Land

Dana Meachen Rau

7421

mc Marshall Cavendish
Benchmark
New York

Earth has lots of land. Land can have lots of trees. It can be dry and rocky. Land looks different wherever you go.

The seven large land areas on Earth are *continents*. Asia is the largest continent. Australia is the smallest.

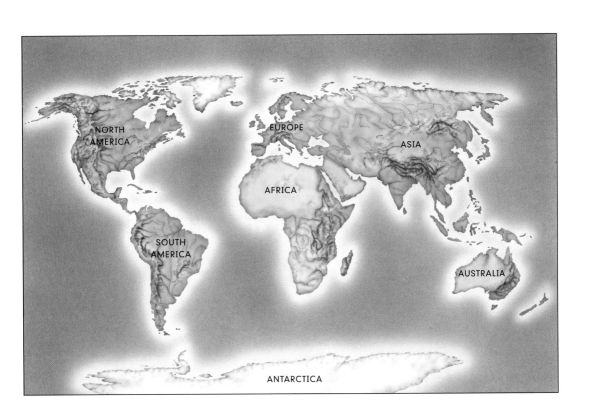

Continents have mountains.
The tops of mountains are
high above the ground.
Mount Everest, in Asia,
is Earth's tallest mountain.

Plains are flat areas of land.
Hills and *valleys* are high and
low areas of land.

Caves are holes in the land
that go deep underground.

Farmland is covered with soil.

A seashore is covered with sand.

Water and wind change the land. This change is called *erosion*. A river of water cuts through the land. The water even wears away the rock.

14

Wind blows away soil and sand. Wind makes *dunes* on a beach.

The continents are on Earth's thick *crust*. The crust is made of hard rock. It has many separate parts.

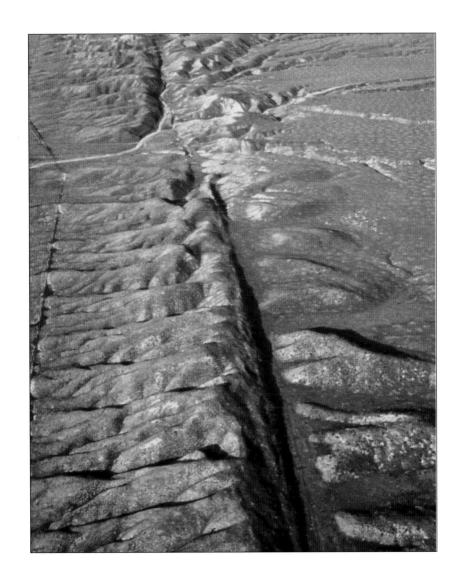

These parts of the Earth's crust can move. When they rub together, this makes an *earthquake*.

Earthquakes make the ground shake. They can knock down buildings.

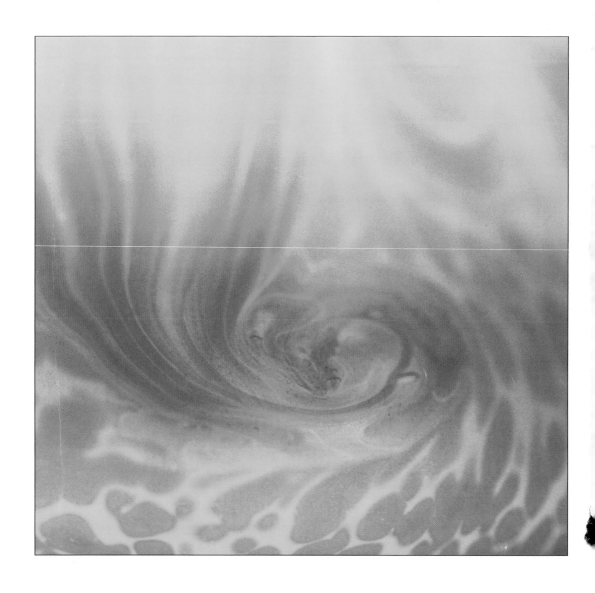